The Calypso Alphabet

John Agard

Illustrated by Jennifer Bent

Henry Holt and Company
New York

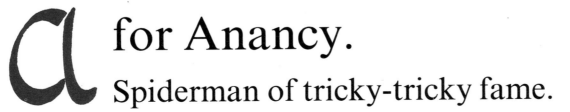

A for Anancy.

Spiderman of tricky-tricky fame.

 for bat and ball.

That's cricket. Play the game.

 for Caribs.

From them Caribbean got its name.

d for doh-doh.

Bedtime, close those eyes.

e for eh-eh!
A sound of surprise.

f for flying fish.

Fins flashing under skies.

 for giddy-up.

Say it to make a donkey hurry.

 for hurry-hurry.

Hurry-hurry make bad curry.

i for iguana.

Watch it dart in a flurry.

j

for jook.

A nail can do this if you play barefeet.

k for kaiso.

Song with a sweet-sweet jump-up beat.

for lickerish.

So greedy all you do is eat-eat.

 for Mooma.

No matter what you call her, she's still Mommy.

n for navel-string.

Bury baby-cord then plant a tree.

 for okra.

Cook with it, wash your hair, it's still slimy.

p for pan.

Beat this steel drum, feel your body shake.

q for quake.

A basket that Amerindians make.

r for roti.

Eat it like bread, flatter than a bake.

 for sugarcane.

It gives sugar and sweet to chew.

t for tanty.

She's your aunty. You don't hear her calling you?

u for ugli fruit.

Grapefruit and tangerine in one.
That's a clue.

 for volcano.

It can blow up like long ago.

 for work-song.

Sing it while you work-o, work-o.

 for Xmas.

Time for masquerade drum and flute to blow.

y

for yam.

Drop it in your soup or mash it with butter.

 for zombie.

A walking dead! No laughing matter.

Notes

Anancy
A popular folk figure who by cunning almost always comes out on top.

bat and ball
Cricket was introduced by the English and the West Indies cricket team has won international renown. There are two teams, each consisting of eleven players. The game is so passionately loved in the Caribbean that children sometimes improvise games using a coconut branch for a bat and even fruit for a ball.

Caribs
One of the Amerindian peoples who inhabited the Caribbean archipelago. With the arrival of Columbus and the Europeans in 1492, despite strong resistance from the Caribs, the indigenous peoples were virtually exterminated from the islands and had to seek refuge on the mainland. Today the Caribbean bears the name of the Caribs.

doh-doh
A term for sleep used in the Caribbean.

eh-eh!
An exclamation of amazement at a strange sight or happening.

hurry-hurry make bad curry
A Creole proverb similar in meaning to ''More haste, less speed''.

kaiso
A common word for Calypso. Calypso music is noted for its satirical humor, political awareness, and vigorous beat.

lickerish
In the Caribbean this archaic English word is used to describe a greedy person.

Mooma
A term for mother heard among the East Indian community of the Caribbean islands.

navel-string
Traditionally a baby's umbilical cord is buried and a tree planted over the spot. The custom shows the connectedness of the child with the earth and its ancestors.

okra (ochroe)
A plant whose edible pods have a slippery texture. It is traditionally believed to be good for hair.

pan
The common name for a steel drum made from an oil barrel.

roti
Made from flour, kneaded into a dough, rolled flat and cooked on a hot iron pan called a tawa. It is usually served with curry.

tanty
A derivation from *la tante* (aunt). It is heard in those parts of the Caribbean where Creole has been influenced by French.

work-song
Found in virtually all cultures and usually sung by groups of people to accompany hard physical work.

Xmas
Masquerade bands are an integral part of Caribbean Christmas celebrations, combining African and European influences. (X is a commonly used abbreviation for Christ, from the Greek letter Chi.)

zombie
According to Haitian folk belief it is someone resurrected from the dead to do the bidding of a sorcerer. It is said that the zombie has neither will nor soul and can break the sorcerer's spell only by eating salt.

Text copyright © 1989 by John Agard
Illustrations copyright © 1989 by Jennifer Bent
Lettering and book design by Simon Bell
This book produced by Beanstalk Books Ltd;
The Gardens House, Hever Castle Gardens,
Nr. Edenbridge, Kent TN8 7ND
Published by Henry Holt and Company, Inc.,
115 West 18th Street, New York,
New York 10011.
Published in Canada by Fitzhenry & Whiteside
Limited, 195 Allstate Parkway, Markham,
Ontario L3R 4T8.
LC:89-045617
Henry Holt books are available at special
discounts for bulk purchases for sales
promotions, premiums, fund-raising, or
educational use. Special editions or book
excerpts can also be created to specification.
For details contact:
Special Sales Director
Henry Holt and Company, Inc.
115 West 18th Street
New York, New York 10011
First Edition
Printed in Italy by Lito Terrazzi, Florence
1 3 5 7 9 10 8 6 4 2
ISBN 0-8050-1177-3